サッカーボール海を渡る

飼牛 万里
かい ご まり

海鳥社

こんにちは。
ぼくはサッカーボールです。
日本の北、東北地方にある小さな町がぼくのふるさとです。
山に囲まれ、青い海に面した美しい町です。

ぼくは、その町の隅っこにあるスポーツ店で、仲間の野球ボールやバレーボール、バスケットボールたちといっしょに、棚の上で毎日のんびりと過ごしていました。

ある日、小学生4、5人が先生に連れられて店にやってきました。

「わー、たくさんあるわね。どのボールにしようかな」

「これにしようよ」

「いや、こっちのほうがよさそうよ」

「じゃあそれにする？」

もう突然の大騒ぎです。

ぼくはびっくりして目をパチクリしていると、スポーツ店のおじさんが、ぼくを棚からおろして女の子に渡しました。

「これにしよう。けんちゃんはサッカーが大好きだし。きっとこのボール気にいってくれるわよ」

「そうだ。そうだ」
みんな大賛成でした。

あっという間にぼくは袋に入れられて、ゆらゆらしながらどこか知らない場所に連れて行かれました。
着いたところは小学校の教室でした。

先生が話しています。
「さあ、これがけんちゃんにプレゼントするサッカーボールです。みんなでボールに記念のサインを書きましょう」

もう、ムズムズ、ムズムズ、くすぐったいやら、こそばゆいったらありゃしない。
ぼくの顔や体に、みんながマジックで自分の名前を書いていくんだから。

翌日も、ぼくは同じ教室にいました。

すると、先生がサッとぼくを持ち上げてみんなに言いました。

「けんちゃんが別の学校に行くことになりました。今日はお別れの日です。みんなで記念のボールをけんちゃんに贈りたいと思います」

悲しくて、けんちゃんもみんなも目に涙を浮かべています。ぼくも悲しくなってしまいました。

でも、みんなからけんちゃんに、ぼくがしっかりと手渡されると、けんちゃんも大喜び。
そしてみんなからも拍手喝采。

「けんちゃん、これからもがんばってねぇー！」

けんちゃんは、ぼくを大切に家に持って帰りました。何度も何度も、ぼくをなでたり、さすったり、抱きしめたり。ぼくもとってもうれしくなりました。

それから毎日毎日、けんちゃんとぼくはいっしょに遊びました。
もう、楽しくって、楽しくって。
家に帰ると、ぼくを大切に網の中に入れて、けんちゃんのベッドのそばにつるしてくれました。
寝ているときも起きているときも、ぼくたちはいっしょで最高の仲良し。
けんちゃんは学校から帰ってくると、決まってぼくのところに飛んで来て
「ただいまぁ」と声をかけてくれました。
けんちゃんは、ぼくを見るといつもうれしそうでした。
ぼくも。
二人とも大切な友だちだったから。

それから何年かたったある春の日の午後のことでした。
窓からポカポカと日ざしがさしこんでいました。
ぼくは気持ちよくうとうとしていると、突然部屋がガタガタと音を立て、家全体が激しく揺れました。

8

あちこちから物がどさどさ落ちてくるし、たんすや机がひっくり返るし。

ぼくは何がなんだか分からずに、ただ震えていました。叫んでも、だれもいません。

「どうしょぉー」ぼくは泣きそうでした。

けんちゃんはどこにいるんだろう。

そのうち窓ガラスが割れ、カーテンが破れ、今まで見たことのないおばけのような真っ黒い水がドォーッと流れ込んできました。

「ひゃあー、助けてぇー！ こわいよぉー！」

ついに家全体がフーッと持ち上げられると、すさまじい勢いの流れの中に飲み込まれていきました。

ぼくは網の中で必死にくぎにしがみついていましたが、どうしようもありません。

とうとうくぎから網がちぎれて、ぼくの体はぐんぐん渦の中に引き込まれていきました。

地面の上にあったものは、ぜーんぶめちゃくちゃに壊されて、巨大な波にどんどん押し流されていきました。自動車もありました。家もテレビも冷蔵庫も。船もありました。木も、花も、犬も、猫も、もちろん小さな虫も。大人も子供も。おもちゃも。そしてぼくも。みーんな流されていきました。

「あぁ、いたい！」
「あぁ、くるしい！」
「あぁ、もうだめだよぉー！」

いろんなものに激しくぶつかりながら、ぼくは必死に水の中でもがいていました。

それからどれくらいたったんだろう。
ぼくは気を失って、水の上にぷかぷか浮いていました。
ふと、なにか小さな声がしました。
「きみ、だいじょうぶかい。あっちから流されてきたんだね。大変だったろ」
カモメでした。
「ここはどこ?.」
「海だよ。きみ、知ってるかい。あっちでとても大きな地震と津波があったんだよ。何もかも壊れて流されてしまったらしいよ」
カモメからそう教えられて、ぼくは急に不安になりました。
「けんちゃんはどうしてるだろう」
心配で心配でたまらなくなりました。

あたりを見回すと、海しかありません。
ぐるっとどこまでも海が広がっています。
その広い広い海のどまん中で、
ぼくはたった一人ぽつんと漂っていました。

「これからどうなるんだろう。
けんちゃんもいないし。誰も助けてくれないし」
ぼくはさびしくなって、悲しくなって、こわくなって
わんわん泣きました。
いつまでも涙があふれてきました。
「つらくて、いっそ海の底に沈んでしまいたい」と思いました。

疲れ果てて、
ぼくは波に揺られているだけでした。

少しずつ日が暮れてゆきました。
ふと見上げると、空が一面黄金色の夕日に染まっています。
そして海も同じ色に染まっています。
空と海がひとつの色に溶け合って、きらきら輝いています。
「わあ、なんてきれいなんだろう！」
ぼくがうっとりしていると、やがて夜がやってきました。
こんなに暗い夜は初めてです。とてもこわくなりました。
そのとき、空の上から声がしました。
「こわがらないで」
それはお月様でした。
高いところからお月様とたくさんの星たちがぼくを見てて、
ぼくを優しく照らしてくれました。

今度は空が少しずつ明るくなって、
お月様は「またあした」と言って見えなくなりました。

かわりにお日様があらわれて、
「ああ、おはよう。今日もいい日にしようね」って
ぼくにあいさつをしてくれるんです。

波がぼくを乗せて、少しずつどこかへ運んでくれているようでした。

海ガメおばさんが寄ってきて、
「ぼうや、どこに行くの？」ってたずねてきました。
「わかんない」ってこたえたら、
「気をつけてね」って言ってくれました。

昼間はよくトビウオのこどもたちがぼくを囲んで、
「いっしょに遊ぼうよ」と誘ってくれました。
飛びはねたり泳いだり、楽しかったなぁ。

ある日突然、こわそうなサメに出会いました。
「お前のような生き物はこれまで見たことないね。食べられるのかな？」

郵 便 は が き

料金受取人払郵便

博多北局承認

0215

差出有効期間
2020年8月31
日まで
（切手不要）

812-8790

158

福岡市博多区
　奈良屋町13番4号

海鳥社営業部 行

通信欄

通信用カード

このはがきを，小社への通信または小社刊行書のご注文にご利用下さい。今後，新刊などのご案内をさせていただきます。ご記入いただいた個人情報は，ご注文をいただいた書籍の発送，お支払いの確認などのご連絡及び小社の新刊案内をお送りするために利用し，その目的以外での利用はいたしません。

新刊案内を ［希望する　希望しない］

〒　　　　　　　　　☎　　（　　　）
ご住所

フリガナ
ご氏名
（　　　　歳）

お買い上げの書店名	サッカーボール海を渡る

関心をお持ちの分野
歴史，民俗，文学，教育，思想，旅行，自然，その他（　　　　）

ご意見，ご感想

購入申込欄

小社出版物は全国の書店，ネット書店で購入できます。トーハン，日販，大阪屋栗田，または地方・小出版流通センターの取扱書ということで最寄りの書店にご注文下さい。本状にて小社宛にご注文下さると，郵便振替用紙同封の上直送いたします（送料実費）。小社ホームページでもご注文できます。http://www.kaichosha-f.co.jp

書名		冊
書名		冊

「いいえ、絶対に、絶対に食べられません。ぼくはサッカーボールです！ おいしくなんかないよ！」
「そうか。じゃあやめとく」と言ってどこかへ行ってしまいました。
「あぁ〜、助かったぁ〜」

ボーっと遠くの海を眺めていた日のこと。
突然、東の方から大きな船が近づいてきたのです。
「おーい、ぼくはここだよぉー」といっしょうけんめい叫びました。
でもぼくの声は、船の大きな音にかき消されてしまいました。
そしてぼくは、スクリューのものすごい勢いに巻き込まれてしまいました。
何度も深い海に突き落されて、ぼくは下へ下へと沈んで行きました。

「もうだめだ」と思った瞬間、暗い海の底で眠っていた深海魚のおじさんが、ヌーっとあらわれました。
騒ぎで起こされたのでしょうか、

「おまえ、こんなところに来るんじゃないよ」とどなってぼくを海面まで放り上げたんです。
やれやれ、もうくたくただったよ。
ぼくはやっとの思いで脱出しました。

それから何日も何日もぼくは海に漂っていました。

海っていうところは、波が穏やかで静かなときは気持ちいいんだけど、
雨や風が強いときは、波も怒っててこわいんだよ。
雨にたたきつけられたり、風で吹き飛ばされたり。
本当にこわかった。
嵐にはさんざんいじめられたなぁ。
逃げても逃げても追っかけてくるんだから。

暑い日もあったよ。
もうぼくの顔がお日様の光や熱でふにゃふにゃになりそうなくらい。
でも海の水で冷やせたからよかった。

反対に寒い日もあったよ。
今度は凍りそうでコチコチになっちゃって。
早くあったかいところに行きたいなぁと思ってた。

ある晴れた日、真っ青な空に浮かぶ雲を見ていると、遠くから渡り鳥の群れがやってきて、ぼくの頭の上を次から次へ飛んで行くんです。
「おーい、どこに行くんだー。
ぼくはひとりここにいるんだぞー」
と声をあげていると、
その中のいちばん小さな一羽が
ふわふわとおりてきました。
「長旅で疲れてるんだ。ちょっと休ませてよ」と言って、ぼくの頭の上にとまりました。
その鳥はホッとしたみたい。

目を閉じてゆらゆらしていました。

しばらくすると、

「あー、助かったよ。少し元気になった。ありがとう。

それにしても、きみ、あちこち傷ついてるね。ここがちょっとへこんでいるし。気をつけてな」と言って、飛び立って行きました。

「元気でな」

ぼくは、その鳥が点になって見えなくなるまで、いつまでも空遠くを見上げていました。

そのとき、ぼくは「ドキッ」としました。初めて知ったんです。ぼくの体が縮んでへこんでいることを。

大変です。

このままでは、空気がどんどん抜けて、いつかは海の底に沈んでしまう。

けんちゃんにも会えなくなってしまう。

けんちゃんとサッカーができなくなってしまう。
絶対にそんなのいやだ。絶対に。
何が何でもそんなのいやだ。
ぼくは自分に言い聞かせました。

それからは思い切って勇気を出して、
いろんな魚や鳥に出会うたびに、
声をかけて必死にお願いをしました。
「どうしても陸地に行きたいんだけど、連れてってくれる？」
「そんなの無理だよ。ゴメンネ」って断られるばかりで。

こうやって、海といっしょに毎日毎日すごしてたんだけど、
けんちゃんのことを思わない日はなかった。
「けんちゃん、元気にしてるかな？」
「またけんちゃんに会いたいなぁ」
そう思うと、いつもひとりで涙をこらえていました。

22

だいぶん時がたったある日、クジラの親子が通りかかりました。
すると、ぼくを見つけて声をかけてくれました。

「私たちはこれからアメリカの北にあるアラスカの方へ行くの。もしよかったらいっしょに行きません？この子も喜ぶわ。
あなた、疲れてるんでしょ。わたしの背中に乗ってもいいわよ」

ぼくはもう、うれしかったのなんの。
お母さんクジラとこどもクジラにはさまれていっしょうけんめいついて行きました。
どんどんぐんぐん泳いで行きました。
ぼくが疲れてしまうと、

こどもクジラが
「だいじょうぶ。がんばって」
と励ましてくれました。

ずいぶん泳いだころ、
お母さんクジラが遠くを指して教えてくれました。
「やっと来たわ。
どう、水平線の上にかすかに陸が見えるでしょ？
あれが、アラスカですよ。
そばまで連れてってあげましょう」

ぼくはいっしょうけんめい目をこらしました。
だんだん近づくと、
白い峰々が連なった陸がくっきり見えてきました。
なんて美しいんだろう！
ぼくは感激で言葉も出ません。

お母さんクジラが勢いよく汐を吹いて、ぼくを陸の方へ飛ばしました。

「じゃあ、お元気で。さようなら」

こどもクジラは大きくジャンプして、さよならしてくれました。

「ほんとうに、ほんとうにありがとう！二人ともお元気で！」

クジラの親子にお礼を言って、ひとりぼくは波に乗って砂浜にたどり着きました。小さな島のやわらかい砂の上でした。

「ああ、やっとここでゆっくりできる」と思ったとたん疲れて眠ってしまいました。

突然、
「あ、これはサッカーボールじゃないか」
という声で目が覚めました。
そこには、ぼくの知らないおじさんが不思議そうな顔をして立っていました。
ぼくを持ち上げて、ぼくの体に書いてあったサインを興味深そうに眺めています。
その時ぼくは思いました。
「ああ、よかった。みんなが書いてくれたサインがまだそのままだったんだ。心配してたんだ、消えてしまわないかって」
おじさんはぼくを抱えて家に帰りました。家で料理をしていた奥さんと、なにやら話しています。

「あら、これは日本から流れてきたボールですよ。あの地震と津波の日から1年かけて、太平洋を5000キロも旅して、ここにたどり着いたんだと思うわ」
と奥さんが、
ぼくの体に書いてある日本語を見ながらおじさんに話しています。

アメリカ人のおじさんの奥さんは、偶然にも日本人でした。
みんなのサインを読んでもらえて、本当によかった。
おばさんは、優しくぼくをなでて、温かいタオルにくるんでくれました。
長い旅の疲れがぬけてゆくようでした。
ぼくはほっとしました。

翌日、おじさんは、ぼくの姿を可哀そうに思って、空気を入れてくれました。

「ばんざい！ やっとぼくはまん丸になりました！」

それから、おじさんとおばさんはぼくの体に書いてある日本語をいっしょうけんめい調べていました。

名前のほかに、日付や小学校名、

そして「けんちゃん、がんばれ!!」とメッセージが書いてありました。

二人とも忙しそうです。

地図を調べたり、パソコンの前に座ったり、電話をかけたり。

ある日、おばさんが大きな声を上げました。

「やっとわかったわ！

これは東北の小さな町に住むけんちゃんのものだってことが。

そしてけんちゃんは無事で生きてるってことが！」

おじさんはそれを聞いて大喜び。
日本の地震のこと、津波のことを知っていたので、
とても心配していたのです。

そばで話を聞いていたぼくは、ひとり涙していました。
「けんちゃんが無事だったんだ。よかった、本当によかった！」

おじさんとおばさんは、
ぼくをけんちゃんにぜひ返したいと思いました。

けんちゃんは津波で、家も何もかもなくしていました。
その後、両親と仮の家に住んでいました。
ぼくが見つかったことを知らされて、
けんちゃんは直接電話で
アラスカのおじさんとおばさんに連絡を取ることになりました。
電話がつながって、ぼくの無事を知ったけんちゃんは大喜び。
もちろんぼくも。

それからひと月して、
おじさんとおばさんはぼくを大切に箱にいれて、
日本行きの飛行機に乗せてくれました。
今度は、ぼくが1年をかけて
波に乗って渡った太平洋のはるか上を飛びながら、
ぼくの心にはいろんなことがよみがえってきました。

とってもつらかったけど、
トビウオのこどもたちと遊んだり海ガメおばさんに出会ったり。
お日様やお月様、星たちがぼくを見守ってくれて。
夕焼けで染められた空と海の中で泳ぐこともできたし。
渡り鳥のこどもが喜んでくれたし。
クジラの親子に助けられたし。
そして優しいおじさんおばさんがぼくを見つけてくれたし。

なつかしい国にやっと帰ってきました。
さっそくけんちゃんが待っている、ぼくのふるさとの町に向かいました。

ぼくはもうわくわくして、そわそわしていました。
けんちゃんはぼくが着くのをまだかまだかと家の外で待っていました。
「けんちゃん、やっと帰ってきたよぉ。会いたかったよぉ」
ぼくは泣いていました。
けんちゃんも同じ。ぼくをしっかり抱きしめてくれました。
けんちゃんは、ぼくを優しくなでて言いました。
「本当にうれしいよ。大変だったね。よく帰ってきてくれたね」
「元気でよかった。また会えてよかった」
さっそくぼくたちはサッカーをして遊びました。
けんちゃんは元気よくけって、ぼくは空高く舞い上がりました。

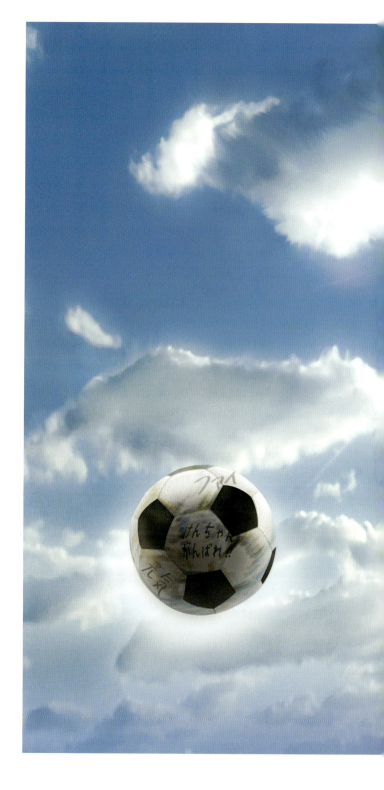

あとがき

このサッカーボールの物語は、実際にあったお話をもとに描いたものです。

二〇一一年三月十一日に起きた東日本大震災のほぼ一年後の二〇一二年四月二十二日付で、ある小さな記事がインターネットに掲載されていました。それを読んだ瞬間、その内容に惹きつけられてしまいました。一個の小さなサッカーボールが、大震災の津波で日本から押し流され、太平洋の大海原を一年かけて漂流し、北米大陸のアラスカに漂着したというのです。しかもそのあと、日本の持ち主のもとへ帰ることができたとのことでした。

私には、戦後まもない子供のころ両親に連れられ、日本とアメリカの間に広がる太平洋を二往復、貨客船で横断した経験がありました。当時、船では片道の横断に約二週間かかりました。来る日も来る日も三六〇度見渡す限りの海。地球の広がりを肌身で感じていたあの時の記憶が一気に呼びさまされ、サッカーボールの物語に心を奪われてしまいました。

「巨大な怒濤に飲み込まれた後、一年も海の上で独りぽっち、

どんなにつらかっただろう、どんな思いだったろう」。いろいろな想いで胸がいっぱいになりました。

でも、独りぼっちだと思っていても、見上げれば月や太陽が見守ってくれています。美しい夕日や朝日が心を包んでくれます。空飛ぶ鳥や海を泳ぐ魚が声をかけてくれるかもしれません。ひょっとしたら自分も声をかけてあげられるかもしれません。そしたらちょっぴり勇気と希望が生まれてくるかもしれません。

私たちの人生には、全く予期しないことが起こることがあります。よいこともあれば突然大海原に放り投げられたように絶望的になることもあります。でも、悲しみや苦しみに沈んでしまいそうになったとき、このサッカーボールのことをそっと思い出してみてください。ボールが荒波にもまれながらたどった五〇〇〇キロの軌跡は、決して消えることはありません。

「よくがんばったねぇ」

私は心の中でボールに声をかけていました。どこかでボールもきっと私の声を聞いてくれていることでしょう。

二〇一九年一月

飼牛 万里

"How could it be possible, spending the harsh days on the ocean totally alone for a year after tumbling through the enormous surge of waves? How hard it must have been for you, ball! How did you feel? What were you thinking during those countless, helpless days?" Soon, I found myself suffused with intimate feelings for the ball.

But imagine, you may think you are alone, but look up and the moon and the sun are watching you. You may find yourself enwrapped by the beautiful light of the sunset or the sunrise. Birds flying in the sky or fish swimming in the sea might say hello to you. You can even call back hello, too. And then, perhaps, you might be able to find a small amount of courage and hope.

In our life, things we had never expected sometimes do happen. Some make us happy or some make us hopeless as if we have been thrust into the wide ocean. But just try, if you can, to think about the soccer ball when you feel desperate with sorrow and pain. The long distance of 5,000 kilometers that the ball trod through the rough waves will never disappear.

"You've really made it, ball!" I voiced the words to the ball from my heart. I'm sure the ball would be listening to my voice somewhere.

Mari Kaigo   January 2019

Afterword

This is a story of a soccer ball based on a true story.

Dated April 22, 2012, roughly a year after the Great East Japan Earthquake took place on March 11, 2011, a small article was introduced on the Internet. The moment I skimmed it through, my heart was caught by the stunning power of the story. It told us that a tiny soccer ball was washed away from Japan into the Pacific Ocean by the colossal tsunami caused by the earthquake. After drifting the expansive ocean for a year, it washed up on the shore of Alaska on the North American Continent. And furthermore, it said, the ball was able to be returned to its owner in Japan.

During my childhood days, not long after the War, I have had the experience of crossing the Pacific Ocean by ship with my parents for two round-trips between Japan and America. In those days, it took approximately two weeks to cross one way. Day after day, what you saw were only waters surrounding you 360 degrees. My memory of the endless stretch of the earth that I had directly felt in those trips was instantly aroused and my mind was riveted to the life story of the soccer ball.

The mother whale and the baby whale were kind enough to help me. And the good couple found me."

I finally came back to my sweet familiar country. Right away, I headed toward my hometown where Ken was waiting for me.

I couldn't wait. I was excited and nervous.

Ken had been eagerly waiting for me outside his home.

"I'm home! At last! I missed you!"
I was crying.
Ken was crying, too. He tightly hugged me.

Then he softly patted and stroked me.
"I'm so happy, pal. You had such a hard time. I'm glad you came back to me. I'm so glad you are all right. We're together again. It's really great!"

And off we went to play soccer together.

Ken happily kicked me high up in the sky.

Sitting near them, I was also listening to the news as tears started to fill my eyes.
"Hurray, Ken is safe and well! I'm so glad. I'm so glad!"

The couple wished to return me to Ken.

With the tsunami, Ken had lost everything, including his home. Since then, he had been living with his parents in a makeshift home.
When Ken was told about me, he decided to make a direct phone call to the couple in Alaska. Ken was so delighted, hearing that I was safe and well. I was, too.

After a month, the couple carefully put me in a box and put me on a plane bound for Japan. This time, I was flying high above the ocean which took me one long year to cross. All kinds of memories started to fill my heart.

"It was not easy at all. But I was able to play with the flying fish and meet the kind sea turtle. The sun, the moon and the stars all looked after me. I was able to swim in the sky and the sea painted together by the sunset. The migrating little bird was happy to perch on my head.

Then, the man and his wife were focused on examining what was written on my body. There were names, date and the name of an elementary school, and even a message that read "Ken, we wish you good luck!"

The two looked very busy, checking the map, sitting in front of a computer and making telephone calls.

One day, the wife exclaimed,
"Finally, I got it, I got it! This is a ball that belongs to Ken who lives in a small town in the Tohoku region. And Ken is alive and well!"

Worried after learning about the earthquake and tsunami that took place in Japan, the husband looked so happy to hear that.

"Thank God, all the names everyone wrote are still with me. I was afraid they might be gone."
The man carried me back to his home.
He was speaking with his wife who was cooking in the kitchen.

"Can you believe this? This is a ball that was washed away from Japan. I think it traveled 5,000 kilometers across the Pacific Ocean after that earthquake and tsunami happened. It took one year to get here."
Reading the Japanese written on my body, she was telling the story to her husband.

And by coincidence, the wife of the American man was a Japanese. "Lucky me! Lucky me!" That's why she could read all the names in Japanese.

Tenderly stroking me, she wrapped me in a warm towel. I could feel all the fatigue from the long journey slowly fading away.

The next day, the husband, feeling sorry for my miserable deflated condition, pumped air into my body. "Hurray! I am all round again!"

Thanking the mother whale and the baby whale, I got myself on the waves and finally reached the shore. I was on the soft sand of a beach on a small island.

"Ah, I can finally rest here" I thought. I felt exhausted and the next moment, I fell fast asleep.

"Hey, this is a soccer ball."
A voice suddenly woke me up.
A man was standing there with a puzzled face.

He held me up and was curiously looking at the names written on my body.
At that instant, I thought,

With all my strength, I followed and swam together in between the mother whale and the baby whale. Wow, were they powerful and swift! When I got tired, the baby whale would encourage me and say, "You'll be OK. Hang in there."

Finally, after swimming a long, long way north, the mother whale pointed far away and told me, "We are finally here. Look, can you see the land vaguely stretching along the horizon? That's Alaska. I will take you there."

I strained my eyes.
As we approached the land, the white peaks of the mountains became clearer and clearer.
"I can't believe this. It's so beautiful! How can I describe this?"

The mother whale, with all her might, spouted and blew me off toward the land.
"OK, dear. Keep well and good-bye."
The baby whale made a big jump and waved me good-bye.
"Thanks so much! I wish you both good luck!"

I dared to ask them.

"I desperately want to go to land. Would you take me there?"

"That's impossible. Sorry."

That's how everybody declined.

I was spending my days everyday with the sea but not a day passed without thinking of Ken.

"How are you doing, Ken? Are you all right?"

"I want to see you again, Ken. I miss you so much."

Thinking about Ken, I was always holding back my tears alone.

One day, after a long time of discouraging efforts, a mother whale and her baby whale passed by. When they saw me, the mother whale called out to me, saying,

"We are now going to the north of America, to Alaska. Would you like to join us? My baby will be delighted to have you with us. You must be tired. You are welcome to hop on my back."

I can't tell you how glad I was.

above, until the bird became a tiny spot and disappeared into the sky.

At that point, with a shock, I suddenly realized for the first time that my body had shrunk and gotten somewhat deflated.

"No way. I can't let myself lose the air inside. If that continues, I will sink to the bottom of the sea. I will never be able to see Ken again. I will not be able to play soccer with him again. That's not going to happen to me. Never. No matter what happens, I'm going to live and survive," I told myself.

Since then, I tried hard to summon every bit of courage I had. Whenever I had a chance to meet any fish or bird, place !

One clear day, when I was looking at the white clouds floating above in the blue sky, flocks of migratory birds came flying from afar over my head.

"Hey, where are you going? I'm alone here."
While I was crying out, one of the smallest birds came fluttering down.

"I'm tired after a long journey. Can I rest here for a second?"
Asking, it perched on my head.

The bird seemed relaxed, eyes closed and swaying on my perch.
After a while, it said, "Ah, you saved me. I think I have recovered my energy. Thanks. By the way, I see you are bruised here and there. And the top is a little dented. Take care."
Uttering the words, it flew away.

"You, too," I said and was looking at the sky far and

appeared, being awaken by the noise while he was sleeping on the dark sea bed.

"Hey, you, don't you ever come here, kid" he growled and threw me up to the surface of the sea.

Whew — at last, I escaped. I was dead tired.

For countless nights and days, I was floating on the waters.

By the way, do you know anything about the ocean?
It feels so nice when the waves are calm and quiet but they become real angry when you have strong wind or rain. The rain will smash you or the wind will blow you off. It's so dreadful. I don't know how many times I was bullied by the storm. No matter how fast I swam away, it would chase and run after me.

Also, there were scorching hot days. My face would become flabby from the strong light and heat of the sun. But it was good I was able to cool myself with the sea water.

On the contrary, there were shivering cold days, too. I would get frozen hard. How I longed to be in a warmer shark.

"Hey, you, I've never seen a creature like you before. Can I eat you?"

"No, no, you can never, never eat me. I'm a soccer ball! I don't taste good!"

"Really? I'm not interested if you don't taste good."

Saying that, he went away.

"Aaah, thank God, I'm SAVED!"

It was the day when I was hazily looking at the ocean far away.

All of a sudden, a big ship came into the view and approached from the eastern direction.

"Hey, I'm here," I screamed and screamed to the top of my voice. But my voice was lost in the roar of the ship. And to make matters worse, I was caught in the tremendous power of the screw.

Again and again, I was thrust down deeper and deeper into the sea.

I felt, "Oh no, now's the end!"

But the next moment, a glumpy old deep-sea fish slowly

"Don't be afraid, my friend."
It was the moon.
The moon and numerous stars were watching me from high above. They tenderly shed light over me.

Then the sky little by little began to switch darkness to light.
The moon said "See you tomorrow" and disappeared.
Instead, the sun appeared and greeted me. "Hey, good morning. Let's make it a nice day, dear boy."

It seemed the waves were slowly carrying me somewhere.

A kind lady sea turtle approached me and asked, "Where are you going, son?"
I answered "I don't know" and she said, "You take good care of yourself, child."

During the daytime, many little flying fish would come to me and invited me to play with them. Jumping and swimming, it was FUN !

One day, out of the blue, I encountered a fearful-looking

"What's going to happen to me? Ken is gone. There's no one to help me."

I felt so lonely, miserable and frightened. I cried and cried with tears flowing down my cheeks.
I felt so sad I even wanted to sink to the bottom of the ocean.

Exhausted, all I could do was to resign myself to the moving waves.

Gradually, the day began to grow dark. I looked up and saw the whole sky painted in a golden color. And not only the sky but also the ocean was tinged in the same color. The sky and the ocean were shining, melted together into one gorgeous hue.

"Oh, how beautiful!"

While I was being enchanted by the sunset, the night was preparing to fall. I had never experienced such a dark night. I was very scared.

At that moment, I heard a voice from above.

How much time passed since, I did not know. I had fainted and was floating on the water when I heard a small voice.

"Are you okay? You were washed away from over there. You must have had a terrible time."
It was a seagull.
"Where am I?"
"You are in the ocean. Hey, friend, do you know that there was a huge earthquake and tsunami out there? I hear that everything was destroyed and washed away."

Suddenly a fear gripped me as the seagull told me the news.
"I wonder how Ken is doing now." I got so worried I could not keep still.

I looked around and saw nothing but the wide ocean. A never ending expanse of water seemed to cover the whole earth.
I was totally alone, floating in the middle of vast stretches of the sea.

Then the whole house was lifted up and swallowed into the tremendous force of the water.

I was in the net clinging to a nail but I was totally helpless. The net finally succumbed and was torn from the nail. I was thrown into the massive swirl of water.

Everything that existed on the ground were all destroyed and washed away in the gigantic waves.
There were boats, cars, houses, televisions and refregerators. Trees, flowers, dogs, cats, and of course tiny insects. Both grown-ups and children. Toys.
And me.
Everything, everything.

"Aaah, ouch!"
"Aaah, I can't breathe!"
"Aaah, I'm finished!"

Bumping into millions of things that were swept away in the swirling water, I was desperately struggling to survive in the water.

became best friends. Whenever Ken came back from school, he would rush to me and say, "I'm home, pal." Ken smiled at me and I smiled at him, too. We were best friends, that's why.

Several years passed by and one afternoon on a spring day, I was having a nice doze in the nice warm sunshine that came in through the window. All of a sudden, the room began to rattle, followed by an enormous tremor that shook the whole house.

Things fell from all directions. Drawers and tables turned.

"What happened? What's going on?" I had no idea.
 I was just shivering with fear.
"Where's Ken?" I screamed but no one answered.
"What am I supposed to do?" I was almost crying.

In a while, window panes were shattered and curtains were ripped. And a black monstrous chunk of water I had never seen before came gushing in.
"Waaaah! HELP! HELP!"

The following day, I was still in the same classroom.
The teacher scooped me up in front of the children and said, "Ken is going away to another school. Today is his last day here and we have to say good-bye to him. Now, let's give Ken our soccer ball as a present."

Ken and everyone looked so sad, with tears in their eyes.
I was sad, too.

But when everyone handed me over to Ken, Ken looked so happy. Now everyone was clapping their hands.
"Ken, we wish you good luck!"

Ken held me tight and took me to his home.
He hugged me, patted me and stroked me again and again.
I was happy, too.

Since that day, Ken and I played soccer together every day. What fun it was! When we returned home, he would put me carefully in a net to be hung by his bedside.

Awake or sleeping, we were always together and

I was taken aback by the sudden noise and excitement.

"What's going on?" I wondered. As I was blinking my eyes, the shop owner picked me up and handed me to one of the girls in the group.

"Hey, this one looks cool. Let's take this.
Ken loves soccer and I'm sure he'll like this ball."
"Yeah! Yeah!" everybody agreed.

In no longer than a second, I was put into a plastic bag and taken to a place I did not know.
Swinging in the bag for some time, I arrived at a classroom of an elementary school.

I heard the teacher talking.
"Everyone, so this is the soccer ball we are going to give to Ken as a present. Let's write our names on the ball in memory of our days we spent together with Ken at this school."

"Come on, don't tickle me like that. It's so itchy."
Imagine everybody writing their name with a marker all over my face and body!

H_{i.}

I am a soccer ball.

I'm from a small town located in the Tohoku region in the north of Japan. It's a lovely place, surrounded by mountains and facing the wide, blue sea.

My home was a little sports shop that sat quietly in the back corner of the town. There, I was spending sleepy, carefree days with my baseball, volleyball and basketball buddies on the shelf.

One day, several elementary school children came into the shop escorted by their teacher.

"Wow, so many balls! Which one looks good?"
"I want this one."
"No, this looks better."
"OK, are we going to choose that?"

A Soccer Ball Crosses the Ocean

Mari Kaigo

Kaichosha

世界の隅々に希望の光が届くことを願って

With a wish that a light of hope
may reach every corner of the world

[著者略歴]

飼牛 万里（かいご まり）

上智大学外国語学部卒業。ヴィラノヴァ大学大学院留学。米国とフランスに在住、その他各国を歴訪。福岡アメリカンセンター、駐日米国大使館等の国際機関に勤務。その後長年にわたり、翻訳家、著述家（日本語・英語）及び国際コーディネーター・アートプロデューサーとして活躍。同時に教育者として、多くの教育機関で英語学・国際コミュニケーション論を指導。国際文化交流プロジェクトを専門とする自身の事務所 Globalink 代表を経て、2000年より2016年まで、中村学園大学教授。福岡市在住。主な訳書：「おそれずに人生を」（ビリー・ハワード、講談社）、「海のかいじゅうスヌーグル」（ジミー・カーター、石風社）、「少年時代」（ジミー・カーター、石風社）、「お母さんが乳がんになったの」（アビゲイル＆エイドリエン・アッカーマン、石風社）他多数。英文著書：「The Keeper of the Flame」（海鳥社）。同書はバングラデシュで、ベンガル語に翻訳・出版された。

[About the Author]

Mari Kaigo has had a diverse, cross-cultural experience and professional career, having lived in the United States and France and visited many other parts of the world. After graduating from Sophia University in Tokyo and studying at Villanova University, she has worked for several international organizations such as the Fukuoka American Center and the American Embassy in Tokyo. Later, she has managed her own office named Globalink as a specialist in international cultural exchange projects. She has long been active in working as a translator, writer(both in English and Japanese), international coordinator and art producer. Also as an educator, she has for many years taught English language and intercultural communications at various educational institutions. She has served as Professor at Nakamura Gakuen University in Fukuoka from 2000 through 2016. She currently lives in Fukuoka. Her numerous publications include translations into Japanese of such books as: "Epitaphs for the Living" (by Billy Howard), "The Little Baby Snoogle-Fleejer"(by Jimmy Carter), "An Hour Before Daylight" (by Jimmy Carter) and "Our Mom Has Cancer" (by Abigail and Adrienne Ackermann). She has a book written in English entitled "The Keeper of the Flame" (published by Kaichosha). It was translated into Bengali and published in Bangladesh.

本書出版のため、
惜しみないご支援とご協力をいただきました皆様に、
心より感謝申し上げます。

I would like to express my sincere gratitude to everyone
who has contributed generous support and cooperation
to make this book possible.

サッカーボール海を渡る
A Soccer Ball Crosses the Ocean

First published, February 2019	2019年2月16日　第1刷発行
Copyright©2019 by Mari Kaigo	著　者　飼牛 万里（かいご まり）
Cover & Illustrations by Joko Kubo	装幀・挿画　久保 丈子
Publisher: Masako Sugimoto	発 行 者　杉本 雅子
Published by Kaichosha Publishing Co., Ltd.	発 行 所　有限会社海鳥社
13-4 Naraya-machi, Hakata-ku, Fukuoka-shi,	〒812-0023
812-0023 Japan	福岡市博多区奈良屋町13番4号
Phone 092-272-0120	電話 092（272）0120
Fax 092-272-0121	Fax 092（272）0121
Printed in Japan	印刷・製本　シナノ書籍印刷株式会社
All rights reserved	禁無断転載
	［定価は表紙カバーに表示］

ISBN 978-4-86656-043-4